GARFIELD
and the Spa

Created by Jim Davis
Story by Leslie McGuire

A GOLDEN BOOK • NEW YORK
Western Publishing Company, Inc., Racine, Wisconsin 53404

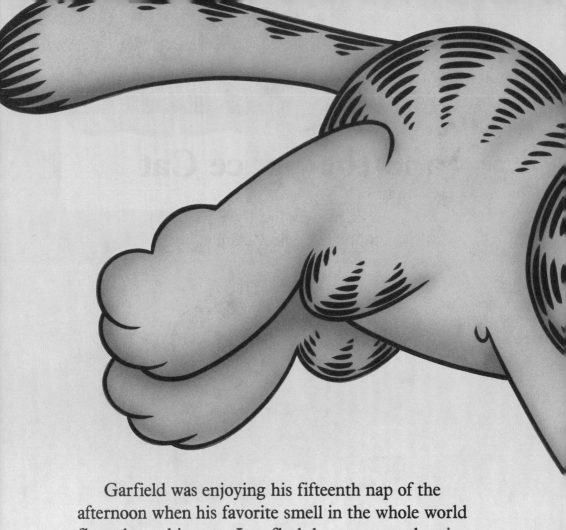

Garfield was enjoying his fifteenth nap of the afternoon when his favorite smell in the whole world floated past his nose. In a flash he was up and racing to the kitchen. Sitting unguarded on the counter was a freshly baked pan of lasagna!

"Say your prayers, lasagna," warned Garfield. "You are about to be gobbled!"

Garfield pounced.

At the last second Jon snatched the pan away. Instead of lasagna, Garfield wound up with a mouthful of countertop.

"No, you don't, Garfield," said Jon. "I'm taking this lasagna to a dinner party."

"I'll get you for this," grumbled Garfield.

Jon tossed Garfield out of the house. "I can't trust you with this lasagna," said Jon. "But if you behave, I'll bring you the leftovers."

"I wouldn't eat your old lasagna if it was the last lasagna on Earth," replied Garfield. "Well, maybe I would."

Still hungry, Garfield decided to check the garbage cans in the alley behind the market. But all he found in the garbage cans was garbage.

So imagine Garfield's surprise when he lifted the last lid and came face-to-face with a cat who looked just like himself, but with two silver antennae sticking out of his head!

"Who are you?" said Garfield.

"I am Fieldgar from the planet Catalon," said the new cat in a crackling, beeping voice. "Who are you?"

"I'm Garfield from down the street," said Garfield. "Do you mean that you're from outer space?"

"Outer, outer space, actually," said Fieldgar.

"What's a space cat doing in a garbage can?" asked
Garfield.

"Garbage can?" said Fieldgar. "This is my stratospace
cruiser. It has four carillium engines and a top speed of
50,000 warps per hour."

"Well, it could use a new paint job," said Garfield.
"Climb out of there and I'll show you around my
planet."

Fieldgar looked around cautiously. "All right," he said, "but we'll have to keep an eye out for the Cosmutts. They've been chasing me across the entire universe."

"We'll be careful," said Garfield, though he didn't know what Fieldgar was talking about.

Fieldgar stopped at the end of the alley. "What are those funny-looking creatures?" he asked.

"Those are people," said Garfield. "They think they run this planet, but we cats are actually in charge."

"We don't have people on Catalon," said Fieldgar.

"Sounds like a great place to me," thought Garfield.

"This is my vet's office," said Garfield. "A vet is an animal doctor. Watch out for people with needles."

"We don't need doctors on Catalon," said Fieldgar. "We cure everything with food."

Garfield really liked the sound of that!

Garfield took Fieldgar home to meet Odie. But when Odie came bounding out of the house, Fieldgar gasped in terror!

"It's an evil Cosmutt!" cried Fieldgar. "Run!"

Garfield grabbed Fieldgar. "That's not an evil Cosmutt," he said. "That's a dumb dog named Odie."

"He looks just like a Cosmutt," said Fieldgar in a shaky voice.

"Too bad for the Cosmutts," said Garfield.

When Odie saw two cats like Garfield, he was even more confused than usual. Finally he decided to give both of them a big, wet lick.

"Yech!" said Fieldgar. "He may not be evil, but he sure is sloppy."

Fieldgar decided that he had better blast back into space before the real Cosmutts tracked him down. He and Garfield were walking back to the garbage can cruiser when suddenly a spaceship shaped like a giant dog dish zoomed out of the sky right toward them!

"Cosmutts!" cried Fieldgar, diving behind a tree.

The spaceship landed in a cloud of smoke and dust.
Out jumped the Cosmutts, who did indeed look just like
Odie. They headed straight for Garfield!

"They think you're me!" Fieldgar shouted. "Take
cover!"

"I can handle these dopey dogs," said Garfield.

"But they'll shoot you with their pasta blaster!" said
Fieldgar.

"What's that?" asked Garfield.

Before Fieldgar could explain, one of the Cosmutts blasted Garfield with something that looked and smelled like warm tomato sauce, cheese, and noodles.

"Poor Garfield!" cried Fieldgar.

"Hey!" said Garfield, licking the messy stuff from his lips. "This tastes just like lasagna! In fact, it *is* lasagna!

"Blast me again!" Garfield shouted to the surprised Cosmutts. "Come on, give it your best shot! Make my day!"

The Cosmutts had never met a cat who could stand up to their pasta blaster. They all yelped as they scrambled back into their spaceship and zoomed away! "Come back!" cried Garfield. "I'm still hungry!"

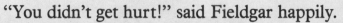

"You didn't get hurt!" said Fieldgar happily.

"On the contrary, I think I gained a few pounds," said Garfield, patting his tummy.

"Thanks for saving me," Fieldgar said. "That was very brave of you."

"I can lick any lasagna in the universe," said Garfield proudly.

When they got back to Fieldgar's spaceship, it was
filled with trash. "Why would anyone put this junk in my
cruiser?" asked Fieldgar, frowning. Garfield tried not to
laugh!

Finally the spaceship was ready to go.

"I'm going to send you a medal for bravery,"
promised Fieldgar.

"I'd prefer a pasta blaster," said Garfield.

With a wave and a roar Fieldgar blasted into space.
"You know, I'm really going to miss him," thought
Garfield sadly. "But not as much as I'm going to miss
those Cosmutts!"

Then Garfield had a happy thought. "Hey, I wonder
if Jon saved me any of that lasagna he made..."